Published in the United
Handmade Public
Ebor House, Troon
South Ayrshire KA10 6JN

C000164359

A CIP record of this book is available from the
British Library
First produced March 2015
Layout and design by Dorothy Gallagher
ISBN 978-0-9932414-0-6

Scarecrow's Dream

Dedicated to fellow scarecrows everywhere

Scarecrow stood in the middle of the field. His head was slumped forwards and slightly to one side, resting on the shoulder of his faded tweed jacket.

The sun had just started its slow climb into the clear blue sky. It warmed the straw that padded out his lumpy sack face, his bumpy body and his long, stiff legs.

This was his favourite time of the day.

But today he did not feel his usual happy self; there was a sadness in him. A sadness that he realised had been there all along but had somehow been forgotten.

A single tear slipped from his button eye and dripped on to the rabbit crouched at his feet.

'Rain?' Rabbit surveyed the cloudless sky.

'Rain?' She questioned the heavens.

Another drop fell upon her, this time landing on her nose. She twitched and looked around her, behind her and then finally above her.

'Was that you, scarecrow?'

She peered into his kind, old face.

'Are you melting?'

Scarecrow shook his head. Losing a few more strands of straw as he did so.

'Not melting,' he sniffed. 'Just remembering.'

'Remembering?' quizzed rabbit.

'What is there to remember? Isn't every day just the same?'

Rabbit nibbled a little more grass then cast another glance skyward.

'Apart from the weather, of course.'

'If you'd asked me that yesterday, rabbit, I would have said 'yes, every day is just the same.' But last night I had a dream and now I'm not so sure.

'I dreamt that I was bigger than I am now and the feeble stick that holds me to the ground was once firmly part of the earth. It belonged there and from it, waves of water flowed up, up, up and through me, making me feel strong and alive.

'I didn't just have two short, heavy arms, but many waving limbs, rich with the greenest, crispest leaves you can imagine. And each one of these arms stretched up to the morning sun, catching its warmth and goodness it its little leaf palms.'

'Oh,' rabbit stopped munching.

'That is a big dream, scarecrow. But why does it make you feel sad?'

Scarecrow sniffed. He tried to speak, but each time he did his words became tears that rolled down his soggy face and onto the ground below.

Rabbit shuffled over to a dry spot.

'Well,' scrarecrow wiped his wet face against the rough cloth of his scarf. 'You see that's not the worst of it, rabbit. When I was this big and beautiful thing, all green and alive and swishing in the wind, I had a purpose, a reason to be…'

'But you have a purpose now, scarecrow. That's why the farmer put you here. Look!'

Rabbit pointed to the bird-filled field next door.

'Without you here, the farmer would lose so much to those pesky birds…and I wouldn't get much peace either,' she added, selecting her next snack.

Scarecrow wailed so loud that rabbit jumped

with fright.

'But that's just it, rabbit. In my dream the birds were my friends. They built their little homes inside my huge, soft arms. I sheltered them from the rain and hid them from danger. I held their little chicks and kept them warm and safe until they were strong enough to balance on my delicate fingers and fly off into the sky.'

'Then one day they returned and built their little homes in me again; they trusted me. I was their friend and my purpose was good. It wasn't meant to be like this.'

Scarecrow dropped his head onto the faded, red scarf that hung around his string neck.

Rabbit tried to think of something useful to say. She started a few times but nothing seemed to work; she didn't even know if scarecrow was listening to her.

Rabbit scurried away. She didn't return to scarecrow's field all day because whenever she thought about him, she felt sad too. But she could not forget his face and the tears that he had shed.

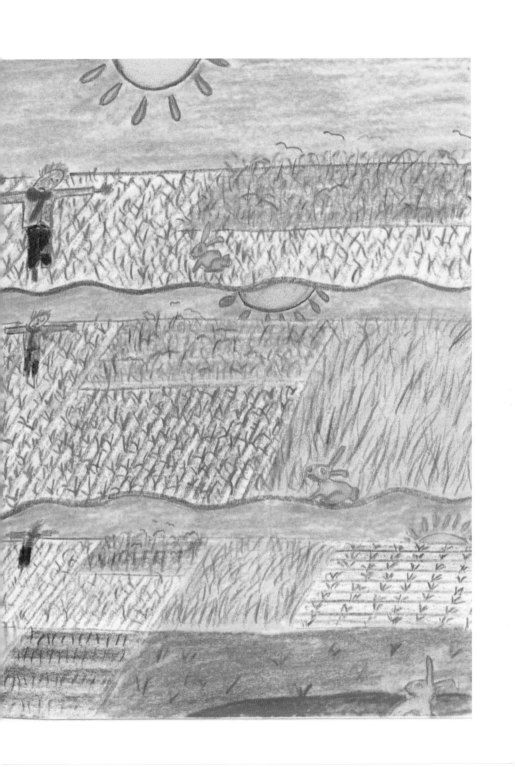

That night, when she settled down in her cosy burrow with all her friends and family around her, rabbit still could not forget scarecrow's sadness.

She thought about him all alone in the field. His only purpose now was to frighten away all the little creatures he had been made to help and protect.

And that night, rabbit had a dream…

The next morning, before the first sparkle of the day had twinkled its way into the burrow, rabbit woke up all her friends and gathered them around her. She told them about poor, sad scarecrow whose true self had been taken from him.

She described what she had seen in her beautiful dream and explained her plan.
Everyone was keen to help and scurried off to make rabbit's dream come true.

For the last hour before the new dawn, they ran

back and forwards between scarecrow's big, empty

field and the nearby woodland. Each rabbit carried

as many leafy twigs as they could manage and it

was the job of the smallest and lightest of paw, to

find each contribution its place on scarecrow's

sleeping body.

When the first warm glow of the sun eased its way above the far horizon, scarecrow felt the heat of the new day warm the thin cloth of his old face. He rolled his head to loosen the hold of the string around his neck and he sighed. He could not forget the dream; it had been with him again all through the long, dark night.

Now that he remembered his true purpose, he did not think that he could ever feel happy in this life again. As the first tear of the day brimmed, he waited to feel it roll down his face. But something was different.

Even with his eyes still closed, scarecrow could see a fluttering around him and the patterns of the sunshine as it danced through, between and beyond a swaying mass.

He felt first one, and then one hundred, soft kisses on his cheeks, and when he opened his eyes, he saw that he was surrounded. A lively cloak of leafy loveliness made from branches, lodged tightly into his tired, old body, swayed all around him, heavy with little green fingers that stretched up towards the rising sun.

Scarecrow squealed with joy and stretched his woody arms to their glorious length. He followed the movement of each branch and saw that it was perfect.

He breathed in the leafy scents and knew that they could bring him life, a life that might once again have true purpose.

It was not long before new roots were formed and scarecrow's trunk and limbs became entwined with the life of the new tree. Birds nestled in his branches and the rabbits, proud of their efforts, made their home beneath his sturdy trunk.

Tree protected them all and they were happy together. And many years later, if you looked deep into the heart of the tree, you could no longer see the old cloth body, the long, stiff legs or the outstretched arms of scarecrow. But you could just, sometimes, see his smiling face.

A face that remembered the way things were before the dream and a smile that told of the wonderful day that scarecrow returned to his true self.